A fabulous soaring thriller.

— *TAKE OVER AT MIDNIGHT,* MIDWEST BOOK REVIEW

Meticulously researched, hard-hitting, and suspenseful.

— *PURE HEAT,* PUBLISHERS WEEKLY, STARRED REVIEW

Expert technical details abound, as do realistic military missions with superb imagery that will have readers feeling as if they are right there in the midst and on the edges of their seats.

— *LIGHT UP THE NIGHT,* RT REVIEWS, 4 1/2 STARS

Buchman has catapulted his way to the top tier of my favorite authors.

— FRESH FICTION

Nonstop action that will keep readers on the edge of their seats.

— *TAKE OVER AT MIDNIGHT,* LIBRARY JOURNAL

M L. Buchman's ability to keep the reader right in the middle of the action is amazing.

— Long and Short Reviews

The only thing you'll ask yourself is, "When does the next one come out?"

— *Wait Until Midnight,* RT Reviews, 4 stars

The first...of (a) stellar, long-running (military) romantic suspense series.

— *The Night is Mine,* Booklist, "The 20 Best Romantic Suspense Novels: Modern Masterpieces"

I knew the books would be good, but I didn't realize how good.

— Night Stalkers series, Kirkus Reviews

Buchman mixes adrenalin-spiking battles and brusque military jargon with a sensitive approach.

— Publishers Weekly

13 times "Top Pick of the Month"

— Night Owl Reviews

# SUNRISE ON 'THE ICE'

## AN ANTARCTIC ICE FLIERS ROMANCE STORY

## M. L. BUCHMAN

Buchman Bookworks

## SIGN UP FOR M. L. BUCHMAN'S NEWSLETTER TODAY

## Other works by M. L. Buchman: *(\* - also in audio)*

# Other works by M. L. Buchman:

## Contemporary Romance (cont)

### Love Abroad
*Heart of the Cotswolds: England*
*Path of Love: Cinque Terre, Italy*

### Where Dreams
*Where Dreams are Born*
*Where Dreams Reside*
*Where Dreams Are of Christmas\**
*Where Dreams Unfold*
*Where Dreams Are Written*

## Science Fiction / Fantasy

### Deities Anonymous
*Cookbook from Hell: Reheated*
*Saviors 101*

### Single Titles
*The Nara Reaction*
*Monk's Maze*
*the Me and Elsie Chronicles*

## Non-Fiction

### Strategies for Success
*Managing Your Inner Artist/Writer*
*Estate Planning for Authors\**
*Character Voice*
*Narrate and Record Your Own*
*Audiobook\**

# Short Story Series by M. L. Buchman:

## Romantic Suspense

### Delta Force
*Th Delta Force Shooters*
*The Delta Force Warriors*

### Firehawks
*The Firehawks Lookouts*
*The Firehawks Hotshots*
*The Firebirds*

### The Night Stalkers
*The Night Stalkers 5D Stories*
*The Night Stalkers 5E Stories*
*The Night Stalkers CSAR*
*The Night Stalkers Wedding Stories*

### US Coast Guard

### White House Protection Force

## Contemporary Romance

### Eagle Cove

### Henderson's Ranch\*

### Where Dreams

## Action-Adventure Thrillers

### Dead Chef

### Miranda Chase Origin Stories

## Science Fiction / Fantasy

### Deities Anonymous

### Other
*The Future Night Stalkers*
*Single Titles*

# ABOUT THIS TITLE

*Reed Walsh* *has been building snowy runways on 'The Ice',*
*as locals call Antarctica, for the last three years. After four*
*months of darkness, two events are about to occur: the first*
*sunrise in four months, and Winfly. The first resupply flight*
*after a long dark winter promises fresh food and new faces.*

*Air National Guard pilot Kathy Lee Forester* *hails*
*from a small town under Montana's Big Sky. When she*
*lands her huge Winfly jet at McMurdo Station, she's*
*surprised by a high school boyfriend grown into a man. But*
*will either of them dare to try climbing that slippery slope*
*of a second chance when the sun rises on The Ice?*

# 1

AUGUST 16TH, IT WAS A DAY FOR CHEATING.

And Reed Walsh did—along with the other thirty-five people who could get away. Halfway between the American McMurdo Station and the Kiwi's Scott Base stood Observation Hill, just a mile from either one. Scott's ill-fated race to be first to reach the South Pole back in 1912 had launched from Discovery Point, close by where the sprawl of McMurdo now stood.

No one here had seen or felt the sun for a hundred and fifteen days. Those bums on the opposite side of the continent along the Antarctic Peninsula didn't count. Some of those bases never completely *lost* the sun.

"Losers! Don't know what you're missing," Reed muttered to himself, with his mouth closed to avoid breathing in the bitter air. It was the end of his third winter on The Ice—as locals referred to Antarctica.

Maybe it was time to move on, though he had no idea why or where he'd go.

He'd feel better tomorrow.

Tomorrow, the sun would leap over the horizon for over an hour for the first time since April twenty-fourth—a date no one on either base had any trouble remembering.

Today, it still wouldn't touch either base, but it might, just might, kiss the top of Observation Hill.

The elevation of both bases was thirty feet above sea level. Just high enough to be clear of the crushing ice that jostled against the southern shore of Ross Island, but not lost in the rough slopes of the inner shore.

The additional seven hundred and fifty-four feet of elevation at the peak of Observation Hill extended the horizon from a mere ten kilometers at the camps to fifty-five. A brief blip of sunlight just might grace Observation Hill. The weather "beakers"—just as cryptic and cautious as any other scientists on The Ice —wouldn't commit one way or the other.

People came in ones and twos from either station, climbing the icy slopes in the chill twilight. August was historically the coldest month of the year. Today's predicted high? Minus twenty-seven degrees but with only a nineteen-degree wind chill—mild by late-winter standards. It was a chilly gamble but that didn't deter many.

Even the chance of seeing the sun was enough to

draw a crowd from the ten winterover Kiwis and two hundred and fifty McMurdoans to the peak. Thirty-five people was a huge crowd by winter standards, especially out of doors.

Reed was the exception rather than the rule. Most winterovers were kept indoors by their experiments: atmospheric this and magnetic that, and telescope the other thing. A lot of the support workers were insiders as well: food, laundry, medical, logistics. They rarely left the cozy interiors except to hustle from one building to the next.

Even in winter, much of Reed's life was outdoors. He'd come to both appreciate the serenity beneath the starry sky, and the alarming view of Mother Nature's immense power. One "day" he'd be watching the snaking lines of the Aurora Australis and the next day the katabatic winds would blast the base so hard that even tight door seals couldn't keep out the ice crystals driven into the vestibules every building had—snow drifts in the dorm entryway were a common problem in winter.

Today was clear skies, the winds were well below brutal, and the temperature merely harsh. He couldn't ask for a nicer day to cheat and leave his job down on the lower ice for a few hours.

Observation Hill was more rock than ice, but not quite the snowless Dry Valleys that lay on the other side of McMurdo Sound. Only three-tenths of a percent of Antarctica was ice-free, and a big section of that lay just a hundred kilometers to the west. In Antarctica's typical strange fashion, the barren areas of the frozen continent were also the driest and deadest deserts in the world.

He loved that kind of juxtaposition. It reminded him of the Montana Front Range almost enough to make him homesick. Bleak winters that never seemed to end and such perfect summer days beneath the Big Sky that it made his heart ache just thinking about it.

One of the other inverted things in Antarctica were the winds. When the katabatic winds sweeping the lower elevations—cold interior Antarctic air draining downward across the glaciers and onto the ice shelves under the force of gravity—were blowing rather than blasting, they split to either side of Observation Hill. There was a strange calm atop the hill itself where you'd expected higher winds. Of course if you were caught up here in a storm, your survival likelihood was very unimpressive even just a mile from base.

And when the katabatics were really on the move —blowing over three hundred kilometers an hour— no one was safe out of doors.

This noontime, people gathered about the rounded peak in twos or threes, but no more than that. After four months of isolation, there was little inner desire to form into larger groups. Though knew everyone here at least by name, he was glad to stand alone at the moment.

Another aspect of The Ice that had fit him down to

his bones. He'd never needed the big crowds to be happy, probably part of growing up in a tiny place like Choteau, Montana. In summer, McMurdo's population rose to almost the same size as his hometown, which was a little crazy as Mactown was also the biggest city on the entire continent.

Today, Reed stood alone by the Memorial Cross. The nine-foot wooden cross had withstood the winds since being erected here in 1912, shortly after the death of Scott and his team attempting to return from the South Pole.

If Robert Falcon Scott could stand where Reed was now, what would he think?

To the west, the light green buildings of Scott Base housed ten in winter and perhaps ninety people in summer. Any of the Kiwi's six main buildings could easily hold the entirety of Scott's famous Discovery Hut—in which sixteen had crowded shoulder-to-shoulder over a final meal before he set out for the South Pole.

And McMurdo? A quarter of the continent's population were based here—whether summer's four thousand or winter's present one thousand. Spread out over thirteen million square kilometers, Antarctica boasted the lowest population density in the world by any measure—by comparison, the Sahara and Siberia were busy places, and the prairie of the Montana Front Range was an intense urban core.

But all the winter peace was about to end. And they all knew it.

For today, they had come to relish the last of the silence.

Tomorrow, the first flight of the year was due with the sun.

All winter, Reed had worked to prepare and maintain the three airplane runways whenever the weather allowed. In mid-winter, it was in case they needed an emergency flight. This had been a lucky year with no emergency med-evacs.

Especially, every survivable day for the last three weeks, he'd been out on the ice doing final prep of the three runways for another year of activity. In the next two months, half of the continent's summer population would arrive, touching down on "his" runways. Ever since he'd built his first runway twenty years ago at eighteen, he'd loved that ownership. Watching the planes come down out of the sky and land safely because of something he'd help build was one of the best highs there was.

Here in Antarctica, the real summer work didn't begin until October, but August was when the early crews began arriving to prepare for the others. Just like always, his runways had to be ready so that the first-wave prep teams could even arrive. Out on the edge was where he'd always belonged.

Winfly—the first supply flight after a long winter— had finally found a hole in the weather. Tomorrow, he'd be down on the Ross Ice Shelf handling the traffic of the first incoming aircraft.

For now?

He turned his face to the northern horizon and waited.

Venus and Jupiter faded completely from the sky until the entire overhead arch shone with an iridescent blue.

The horizon turned a brilliant pink then a soft gold that he had forgotten even existed in the colorless world of The Ice.

The sun haloed the great twelve-thousand-foot massif of Mount Erebus, the world's southernmost active volcano, that rose thirty klicks to the northeast. The few steam clouds above the volcanic caldera burned like a brilliant torch, lighting the whole expanse of Ross Island as the sun caught them. Reflections of sunlight even created shadows across the hummocked ice shelf for the first time in four months.

Actual shadows!

He started to turn to see if it was bright enough to cast his own shadow—

Then, like a mighty spear launching over the horizon, the tiniest edge of sun snuck aloft above Mt. Erebus' shoulder and the distant waves of the Antarctic ocean beyond.

It shone for just five minutes, lighting the entire peak.

Not a word was spoken on Observation Hill.

The only sounds were the low moan of the wind and the sighs of those greeting the sun.

Four months.

Just four months and he'd forgotten the feel of the sun's warmth—the tentative heat—as it brushed his wind-chapped cheeks softly as a kiss.

## 2

ALL THREE MCMURDO AIR STRIPS WERE OUT ON THE Ross Ice Shelf.

Willy Field was as good as permanent, tucked deep on a slow-moving section of the ice. But it lay an awkward distance from the bases and it was strictly a skiway—only planes with skis could land there.

The big, wheeled jets had two options.

Phoenix Runway was far better named than the Pegasus Runway it had replaced. Built on stable blue ice, but it lay almost fifteen kilometers from the base. The ten feet of ice, overlayered with tightly compacted snow, was the only snow runway in the world certified for heavy wheeled aircraft.

The Ice Runway was built anew each year on faster ice close by McMurdo.

And by mid-summer each December, it slid out to sea as the Ross Ice Shelf broke up and melted. By June, the ice shelf would have extended once more, eventually reaching six feet thick, and it was his team's job to carve a new runway there. It was the main field for ingress to Antarctica. After it broke up, the flights moved to the logistically more awkward Phoenix and Willy's.

There was something about the ephemeral nature of the Ice Runway that had always tickled Reed. All those years he'd spent building for permanence and durability under massive loads had become a battle for the ephemeral.

This was Reed's third year overwintering on The Ice, and the third year he'd worked on the runways.

Reed had driven snow blowers, graders, and heavy rollers back and forth over the ice of all three runways until he wondered why he'd left the family's eastern Montana farm in the first place. Plowing back and forth, back and forth until it was perfect.

He did his best not to think about the eighteen hundred feet of water that began just six feet below.

The McMurdo Ice Runway was actually two runways in an X-form to take best advantage of the winds. Both were ten thousand feet long and a hundred and fifty wide, it was as hard as concrete for landing "heavies."

And the C-17 Globemaster III setting up on final approach was the definition of a heavy.

He'd been nervous driving an eighty-ton tractor and its roller on the ice—at least until it became as mind-numbingly mundane as the bitter temperatures. But the plane weighed three *hundred* tons.

The first Winfly of the year was inbound from Christchurch, New Zealand, the land from which all things flowed to McMurdo.

Until it was down, there was nothing more to do but wait and watch. The cargo crew had been huddled in the galley building's warmth until the last moment. He hadn't wanted to risk missing the first plane to touch his new ice. He'd even taken a last walk up and down the runway, looking for any faults that might have impossibly formed since he'd last checked it.

He was only just back to the galley building, now clearly visible in the bright twilight, when he first spotted the black dot.

It rode wide of Mount Erebus, following the western arm of the Ross Sea. It was two months too soon to be a skua flitting toward their summer breeding grounds.

He blinked and lost it in the bright twilight.

Blinked again and it was back.

It was impossible to look away.

Forever small, it didn't seem to grow—until it was very close. Then it was freaking *huge*, and just kept growing bigger. It kissed down with a puff of snow, and settled with a slow grace, as if its pilot was unsure of the ice as well.

It was the second-largest jet in the American military fleet and it swelled as it raced down the runway toward where he and the airfield crew waited. In the last moments it was so big that it blotted out Mount Erebus itself.

Yet the silence remained impenetrable. A brisk wind at their backs and the idling jet engines made it impossibly noiseless.

The next instant, everything was a flurry.

With the reversers engaged, the engines roared to life shattering the pre-dawn quiet. Snow swirled and painted the turbulence spinning off the plane in great white swirls.

When it was finally slow and close, everything calmed down.

He could just spot the pilots perched high above as they carved a tight turn to point back down the runway. At last, it cycled down the engines and the quiet returned. Over the next four months, until the ice became too unsafe due to breakup, forty flights would land here. But the first was always special.

With a whine of hydraulics, the rear ramp split wide—half folding up into the plane and half slanting down onto the snow.

The next instant, with an abruptness that always rocked him back on his heels, winter ended.

First came the burst of excited voices—each one alone more charged with energy and sheer volume than the entire base's population combined had probably mustered in the last two months.

Riding on the wave of chatter, "orange people"

poured down the rear ramp. Each was dressed in a Big Red. The only thing out of place about their monster parkas was how fresh and unused they were. But their skins were...so tanned.

He glanced over at Simon, another airporter.

They exchanged a quiet nod, both remembering the same conversation.

"Hey, by the end of the winter even a black dude like me will turn pasty white." While Simon's dark skin hadn't quite done that, it was still accurate. No one on base had even a hint of sun-tone to their skin.

No words needed, they traded a smile—then dodged aside as the mob stormed Ivan the Terra Bus for the three-kilometer drive over the ice to the base. Simon was a first-year and had taken over as cargomaster. It was his job to unload the big plane under the watchful eyes of the C-17's loadmasters.

Reed wouldn't miss that job one bit. Instead, he carried his instruments to the airplane tires and rigged up the sensors.

The runway might be as hard as concrete but it wasn't concrete; it was ice. And ice wasn't a solid—it flowed.

He'd spent a long quiet evening with a physics beaker talking about whether there was such a thing as a true solid. The scientist insisted there wasn't, that even a bar of iron would flow with time, if it didn't rust out first. When Reed had argued about that not making any sense, he'd gotten a lecture on molecular bond slippage. A rock beaker, a geologist, had joined in and posited that crystalline bonding configurations— in any form from diamond to quartz—was so resistant to bond slippage that it must be counted as a true solid.

When the two scientists started in on molecular orbitals versus electron clouds, Reed had given up and gone for another "beaker"—of beer.

All that mattered in his world was that ice was a semi-solid. Leave a half-million pounds of airplane sitting on one spot and the ice would flow from that pressure alone, no matter how cold it was.

His sensors would track the sinkage rate and sound a loud alarm if the plane sank more than ten inches into the ice. Then they'd have to get out a tractor and shift the plane enough to park at a fresh spot on the "solid" surface.

After it was gone, there would be hole-filling and more work with the roller.

For now, he set, calibrated, and tested his equipment.

He was just finishing up with the nose wheel when someone came up beside where he knelt.

"You make sure my plane stays afloat," a woman's voice.

"Yes ma'am. No sinking your plane to the bottom of McMurdo Sound. Gotcha."

Tapping the "Active Monitor" mode on the last sensor, Reed made sure it was synced to his phone, then he turned to look up at her.

He didn't get a look at her face inside her Big Red's furred hood.

He didn't even get to the crisp newness of the Big Red.

Reed never got past the splash of bright yellow held in her heavy mittens.

"A banana? I'll marry you for a banana."

She handed it over.

"Oh my GOD! Freshies! I forgot what they even looked like. It's so...yellow!" He sniffed its length like a fine cigar and sighed happily.

"Are you planning on eating that or falling in love with it? Should I be jealous? You did just offer to marry me after all."

"Eat now! Marry later." Then he briefly hugged it to his chest in his heavily gloved hands.

Her laugh seemed to spill out on the ice, but rather than freezing, it floated away like...like...snowflakes. The capability to build outer-world metaphors was but one of many things that died after spending a full winter on The Ice.

Reed tore open the top and peeled back just enough for that perfect first bite when the laugh registered.

He froze. Unable to move even as much as his Ice Runway, Reed peered upward, trying to see inside her furred hood.

Then he finally recalled when he'd last heard that laugh.

A decade ago, on a warm moonlit night, in a land so far away he wasn't even sure it still existed—though he'd spoken to Mom just last week.

The breath was knocked out of him in a crystalline cloud, "Kathy Lee Forester."

## 3
———

Kathy knew who it was the moment he said her name.

It was the same way he'd said it when he'd picked her up in his Dad's Chevy Silverado 2500 Dually pickup for the senior prom and first seen her in her dress. It *had* been a killer dress. She'd hoped that it would floor him, but she hadn't expected that tone of wonder—then or now.

"Small world, Reed," she couldn't help laughing again.

He just nodded like a puppet—the hood of his oil-stained Big Red bobbing several times. The silence stretched until it was getting a little strange.

"Are you going to eat that before it freezes? I risked my life taking a piece of fruit out of the first delivery stores. But I wanted to bribe whoever was keeping my plane safe."

He bit down on it but she wasn't sure if he even tasted it. He'd also bitten a clump of his furred hood along with it. After he'd dug out the furry bits, he did groan with delight.

"Oh, that's so good! Awesome bribe. Just for this, I'd keep your plane afloat even if it wasn't my job."

He shoved back his hood, which didn't reveal much more of his face, he wore sunglasses and a thick hat pulled low. But she recognized the smile as he took another bite.

"You're looking good, Kathy Lee."

She tried to look down at herself but couldn't even see her feet with the bulk of the Big Red. "I look like the Stay-Puft Marshmallow Man in the old *Ghostbusters* movie. Only fire-alarm red."

"Sorry, Kathy Lee. You're one of those people who can never look less than amazing. Though at the moment it's probably because you're the first outsider I've seen in four months. You know, nothing at all to do with you probably still being gorgeous under all that."

"Same old Reed."

"Same old," he agreed with that easy confidence that he wore so easily. After he finished the rest of the banana, he rolled up the skin neatly and tucked it in a pocket. Then he glanced up at her, reading her silence as easily as he always had. "I'm saving it either because it's illegal to throw away anything anywhere in Antarctica, guys aren't even allowed to make yellow snow here. Or it's because I might want to pull it out and smell it later."

"I brought two *tons* of freshies," she waved at her plane.

"Is that all?" His sadness was dramatic. "I'm definitely hoarding my banana peel."

She couldn't help it; he always made her laugh. Though a little more awkwardly this time. Memories, lots of memories were flooding back.

She'd skipped graduation, leaving for Basic Training the day after the prom—with no sleep. Not because they'd made love all night. Instead, after the dinner and dance, he'd driven her out deep into the emptiness of the prairie far from the town's lights. There they'd sat, hip-to-hip in the truck bed, together until dawn had lit the Big Sky. They'd watched the stars and talked of dreams.

Reed was the only one who never laughed at her dreams. And he didn't just cheer her on; he'd always kept pushing her to think bigger and aim higher.

Their last night together was still one of the best nights of her life. Only now did she know how much she'd missed it.

He pushed to his feet and nodded toward the C-17. "Yours?"

"US Air National Guard Lieutenant Colonel Forester at your service."

"Damn! Definitely making me feel small. That's my

big rig." He waved a hand toward a heavy-duty, tracked Caterpillar tractor still rigged with the big roller.

"Building runways on the Antarctic sea ice. Not *too* shabby even if you *are* still just driving a tractor," she teased him.

He shrugged, as if it was nothing. Dad, who was still the high school basketball coach, had kept her up-to-date on the various boys of the town. He'd said something about Reed. Actually, now that she thought about it, he'd *often* said things about Reed over the years.

"Red Horse?" The memory seemed right.

Reed nodded easily. "And now here. Seem to have runway building in my blood."

"That's seriously impressive." The US Air Force Red Horse was the service's fast-construction squadron—working *anywhere.* Schools after hurricanes, hospitals in Third World jungles, and runways in active battle zones. "Build any runways I might know?"

"Bunch in the Dustbowl. Most were graded for the C-130s, but we did a couple that could handle this beast," he nodded toward her plane.

The construction crews in Iraq and Afghanistan had always amazed her. They went into areas close behind the Army's 75th Rangers. There they built runways, often under active fire, so that C-17s like hers could land. The Air Force needed the runways to deliver the personnel and equipment to properly secure the area—a luxury Red Horse Squadrons rarely had.

"I dumped out early. Figured Master Sergeant was high enough for any mere Montana farm boy. Guess you had different ideas."

"Dumped out early?" Dad had said...what? Oh! That Reed was medically retired after being badly shot up, but if he wanted to downplay that, she understood. Well not really, but—

"Yeah," again that easy signature shrug that barely moved his Big Red before he moved right to another topic. "How long are you on The Ice?"

"Unload and go, about an hour."

Reed stared over her shoulder for a long moment, then shook his head. "Gonna be closer to two. Part of the cost of being the first Winfly plane. Simon and the boys don't have the kinks worked out yet. And they're still moving winter slow. Besides, we've got the first hundred tons of waste to load for you to haul back."

"Winter slow?" She watched the ground crew and they were moving about a third slower than all of the newbies around them. "Does it really do that to you down here?"

"That's them on the hustle. You look a little like you're vibrating with energy to this OAE."

"OAE?" She looked back at him.

"Old Antarctic Explorer. It's a high calling that only the noble few achieve."

She couldn't stop the snicker, which turned to a

laugh as he slapped a thickly gloved hand to his parka-covered chest. Actually, OAE looked damned good on him, like he was right in his element. It was easy to picture him setting out for the South Pole with nothing but a pack and skis.

"To you outer-worlders it means doing a couple summers down here. What it really means is someone who's done a winterover. A year on The Ice. Now some domies—the folks as winterovered down at the South Pole, especially before the station dome was replaced in 2003 for old age—they insist that OAE means you've wintered *there,* but that's just being snooty. Ask any McMurdoan."

"Are we just going to stand out here on the ice all day?" Not that she wanted to run away from Reed. But the cold was punching through her Air Force boots and only two layers of socks. And the tip of her nose wasn't incredibly happy either, despite still having her hood up.

# 4

_____

REED SQUATTED DOWN TO INSPECT THE NOSE GEAR subsidence monitor. Less than a quarter inch so far, which was a good sign. In the summer, when the air warmed the ice from minus twenty to plus twenty degrees, it would be a different story.

And the plane was weighing less with each passing minute that Simon and his crew ran out the pallets of cargo.

He checked that it was reporting properly to the app on his cell phone.

It also gave him a moment to catch his breath.

Lt. Colonel Kathy Lee Forester had been his ideal —something he hadn't realized until she was gone. She'd always had the brains; gone ROTC at some fancy out-East college. He'd been two weeks into summer working Dad's farm when it had struck him like a physical blow—this was what the rest of his life would look like.

Reed had always worked weekends and summers on the farm, could drive a garden tractor by the time he was six and a combine by twelve. But farm time had always been bounded by school. Now he was eighteen, greasing the bearings on the well pump for the irrigation system, and he could wake up in sixty years still doing the same thing.

It had taken him a week to carefully break the idea to his parents. Ma had merely smiled but Dad had snorted out a big guffaw right at the dinner table.

"Wondered how long that would stay stuck in your craw." He'd driven Reed down to the Armed Forces Career Center in the Holiday Village Mall in Great Falls the next day. "You're good at farming, but a blind horse could see it wasn't in your blood. Your Ma said to keep my trap shut until you saw it for yourself."

After chatting for a bit, the recruiter had made a call then sent him five kilometers down the road to Malmstrom Air Force Base, the home of the 819th Red Horse Squadron. It hadn't taken ten minutes talking to the team for him to realize he'd found his future.

At least until he'd been building a school in rural Honduras that ended up in the middle of a drug battle. Two months in the hospital and learning to walk again had taken—

That memory drove him back to his feet.

"We've got a galley over there," he pointed out one

of the shacks on skids that lined this corner the airfield.

"Coffee sounds good," Kathy started walking over. Her walk was different: precise, no wasted motion. Her years in the military *had* changed her.

"Then you haven't had our coffee," which earned him the laugh he hadn't known he missed. He tried to jar things loose inside his brain. Kathy Lee at eighteen and the woman now walking across the bright Antarctic ice beside him twenty years later probably had little in common.

He glanced back to check on Simon, but everything looked to be on track. The base's big-wheeled Foremost Delta II flatbeds were lined up beside the plane. The forklift was lifting pallets as fast as the C-17's loadmasters could shuffle them off. They'd already staged the long line of drums of return cargo on the ice.

Everything was bustle and they didn't need big headlights to see what they were doing.

And in the middle of it was...this woman.

"What's the rest of it?"

For a moment he wondered if she'd turned mind reader, but then noticed her hood turning to scan the other "buildings."

So, to avoid thinking about her, he played tour guide, explaining each item. Fuel tanks, tool shed, emergency shelter in case the weather slammed down and it was too dangerous to try and cover the three kilometers back to base. The shelter was complete with a two-week food and heating fuel supply because, yes, storms could be that bad.

"And it's all on skids so that we can tow them away before the ice melts out from under them this summer."

"You live in a very different world, Reed."

He opened the galley door, which opened into a tiny plywood vestibule. They crowded in together—two people in Big Reds made the space surprisingly small and intimate. He closed the outer door and opened the inner one quickly.

"We've got coffee, tea, and cocoa. The cook's made us donuts this morning. And..." his eyes focused on the table. There was a mound of color on the table, "Freshies!"

"You really missed those, didn't you?"

Reed shed his parka and hung it on his usual hook. "You have no idea. It's the main topic of conversation for the final two months of a winterover." He took an orange. It was even oranger than the banana had been yellow.

"Not stuffing your pockets?"

"Hey, I'm no freshie hog. It's really bad manners down here, about the worst crime there is." He poured two coffees and turned to ask how Kathy Lee would like hers.

No words came out.

She *definitely* wasn't the girl in the clingy dress. Her

long dark hair was now in a neat slice at earlobe length. The dress—his last and most enduring image of her—was now a green flightsuit and a lieutenant colonel's silver oakleaf. Even her face had grown up. The only thing that hadn't changed were those honey-brown eyes. And her laugh.

"Okay. I was wrong. You *never* looked this good. All grown up looks damn good on you, Kathy Lee."

"Kathy."

"Um...nope. Kathy Lee to me. Sorry, you're stuck with that."

The smile hadn't changed either.

# 5

"You never married," the words slipped out. Dad would have told her if he had.

If she drank a third cup of coffee—which wasn't all bad, but definitely needed a heavy dose of real cream rather than the powdered stuff—she'd be even more jittery than she was sitting across the battered wooden table from Reed in the ten-by-sixteen-foot cabin.

They'd covered a lot of old times and newer ones. And even the hard memories had felt easier shared with someone who'd been there and done that.

"Marriage doesn't work when you're in Red Horse Squadron. Had a couple of times where I thought it might be headed that way, then I'd get deployed and get the 'Dear Reed' before I was half done."

"And since?" She'd forgotten how easy it was to talk to Reed. He'd been the same way in high school, even if it took her until senior year to discover that about him. You asked a question and he just answered.

"Been mostly on The Ice. Good place to clear my head. Not such a hot place for meeting women. Gender ratio down here is just as whacked as it is in the military. You?"

She stared down at her hand. The ring was long enough gone that she couldn't see any sign of it...but she could still feel it.

"For a while, but it didn't end well." *He* said it flat out.

"Damn you, Reed. After twenty years, you aren't supposed to be able to read me like that."

"Doesn't take a genius, Kathy Lee. Clearly he was an idiot."

She fooled with her empty coffee mug, "What makes you say that?"

"Duh! He let you go."

"Actually, I threw him out."

"Because he was dumb enough to let you go."

Kathy sighed. Because she'd been turning a blind eye for too long. He was ex-military—turned contractor. And he'd begun crossing moral lines that shouldn't have been possible, that *weren't* possible if she was going to remain married to him.

Her radio squawked for the first time since landing.

"Loading the last of it, Colonel. Fifteen to tie it down, then we're ready to go."

"Roger." Then she turned to Reed. "That's my cue."

He simply gathered up their mugs, the orange peel and the tiny bit of the apple core he hadn't eaten, and cleaned them up. He didn't say a word.

She opened her mouth to say...she didn't know what.

Before she could, the doors slammed open and a blast of Antarctic cold smashed the heat out of the room.

"Coffee!" "Donuts!" "Heat!" "Oh my God, Reed left some freshies for us. You feeling okay, big guy? Thought you'd have scarfed the whole pile when you didn't come out to help." The last one came with significant eye rolls toward Kathy that she couldn't have missed if she tried.

"Didn't want to watch you tripping over yourself trying to load a damned pallet, Simon." Reed shot back easily.

"Hey, whose Big Red is on *my* hook? Shit, summer folk have definitely arrived." Simon picked up her coat and moved it to the next hook. Then he apparently realized what he'd said and offered her a wink of apology.

As the other three members of the cargo crew took off their coats, her own was shuffled from hook to hook until Reed grabbed it away and handed it to her.

The small galley now felt incredibly crowded and she was only too happy to escape back onto the ice.

"Real damn good to see you, Kathy Lee," Reed spoke softly as they walked toward the plane.

"You mean that?"

"Better check your flight carefully, just to make sure I didn't let it sink down into the ice just so you can't leave. I'm most of the way to discovering I like the woman even more than the girl."

Which she decided was one of the nicest compliments she'd ever gotten, even from Reed.

She tested her own feelings,

It had been *beyond* good to sit with Reed. She couldn't understand how two hours had felt like so few minutes.

Reed the boy had been charming. Reed the man, well, he really didn't need anymore adjectives than that. There was a steadiness about him that felt as reliable as the Montana soil.

She tried to see his expression, but he'd yanked his hood up with a certain viciousness as they'd left the galley.

"I'll be flying in another five loads over the next month."

"Uh-huh," he even sounded angry.

## 6

REED STARED DOWN AT THE SNOW AND *KNEW* HE WAS being an utter shit about it. Something Kathy Lee definitely didn't deserve.

Then he looked up at that damn big plane. Just like her high school dreams that night after the prom, he could feel her damn big dreams pulling her away. And he was helpless to stop her.

"Sorry. Being pissed that you're leaving isn't exactly the most constructive thing I've done lately. Not your damned fault."

He forced himself to look at her and held out a hand, "It was *amazing* to see you again, Kathy Lee. Have a safe flight."

She looked down at his hand, but didn't take it. Apparently even that was too forward. It was a good thing he hadn't given voice to any of his other thoughts, like he'd give up most anything just to see

33

her again. And he'd give almost as much to *never* see her again. A two-hour glimpse of her was as much a cruelty as a pleasure.

"Well, uh, I've got to go strip the monitors off your wheels." He made it three paces before she called out his name. For a moment, he wondered if she really had. Between the Big Red's hood and the rising wind, it was hard to be sure.

"Reed!" He could hear the military snap in her voice even if she didn't give it the full command oomph. That too was new.

He forced himself to stop but he couldn't turn to her. She wasn't the girl who had taught him in a single night to dream bigger than the farm. Kathy Lee had become so much more than that. Maybe she really was just Lieutenant Colonel Kathy Forester now.

She walked over and circled around to stand in front of him. Her hood was shoved back enough that he could see her face and her brilliant brown eyes as they shone with the last of the sunlight, now skidding across the snow under the plane's fuselage. He'd missed most of the first day's sunlight. God, and it didn't even matter.

"I hit twenty years."

"More than I did."

"I'm retiring from the military."

"Why? That doesn't sound like you, even a little." Or maybe it did. Kathy Lee was always the girl with a dream. "What's next?"

She pointed south.

He followed the long shadow of her arm stretching across the ice. The only thing south from McMurdo was Amundsen-Scott South Pole Station a thousand kilometers away.

"Say what?"

"I'm retiring in two weeks. Kenn Borek Air offered me a seat. You know they're the top cold-weather pilots anywhere. Antarctica in the southern summer, Arctic between times."

"So I get to see you flitting by every now and then." That was going to be the worst-case scenario of them all.

"You know runways."

"Uh-huh."

"And machines," she nodded toward his Caterpillar tractor. "Knowing you, you can rebuild them if you have to."

"If it's got an engine, I can fix it." He looked up at the two big turbine engines dangling off the wing overhead. He nodded upward, "Well, not that."

Now it seemed to be Kathy Lee's turn to look away. "Uh..."

Reed waited her out. There was some sort of idea forming, he could feel her doing it, but he couldn't figure out what. She was always that one step faster. He loved her ideas, had followed her into the Air Force twenty years ago, but he wouldn't have thought up doing that on his own.

"I..." she kicked at a low snowbank he'd plowed aside not two days ago.

Then she looked him square in the face. Her face wasn't filled with ideas and excitement as she'd been all of those years ago when she talked about the future. But he couldn't read the emotion that had replaced them. He sighed. That too was new.

"Borek Air might have mentioned in the final interview that they need a general hand. Loader and so on, who could also be a mechanic's assistant. They'd probably pay for the A&P license if everything worked out."

He'd thought about getting his Airframe and Powerplant license a couple of times, but never quite found a reason to. He'd certainly helped out on any number of repairs—back when he was still a Red Horse—after a plane was shot up, and they had to get it off one of his runways.

"Huh." It was all he could manage.

Working for an outfit like Kenn Borek, with his knowledge of the cold and adding on an A&P, that would fit him right down to the bones. The Ice had drawn him because he'd never been here. Once here, he hadn't found a reason to leave. But seeing the Arctic, working on planes, that would be new adventures in new places.

Then his brain finally caught up with what Kathy Lee was asking.

"With...you?"

She nodded just a little too fast.

"I, uh…" He shut his trap before he could say anything too stupid.

Her radio squawked again.

"Look," he could hear the military urgency slip back into her voice. "I know it's just a crazy thought. But I'll be back down here five more times with my baby."

"Your two-hundred-ton baby," it was still a little dazzling that Kathy Lee had fulfilled her dream of flying big military jets on such a grand scale.

"Yes. You can, you know, think about it. We can, maybe—" she took a quick breath that looked almost nervous, "—talk. More. Next time. If you want."

"Uh-huh," was all he managed.

"I'll see you later, Reed." She hesitated, then turned and walked away to board her plane. That sharp military stride of the woman who had just looked at him with such…

He laughed aloud and it stopped her in her tracks.

She turned slowly to face him, so silhouetted by the last rays of the first day's sun scooting under the fuselage that she was almost invisible.

Reed walked up to her.

"You were always so fast, Kathy Lee. Hardly ever gave me time to think." He stepped just a little too close and checked her face. Yes, he was right about that expression of hers.

"What are you thinking?" Her voice was no louder than the rising wind.

"I'm thinking..." he wanted to draw it out to tease her, but there just wasn't time.

Her copilot had come looking for her and was waving an arm from the forward passenger door as the rear ramp began swinging noisily into its closed position.

"I'm thinking that having seen you in the Montana moonlight in the most amazing dress known to man, and then in the Antarctic sunrise in a military flightsuit, that I'd really be cheating myself if I didn't get to see you by the light of the midnight sun up north."

And then the tentative look on her face, that look of such hope that their shared perfect moment from the past might somehow become the future, transformed to one of pure joy.

Her hug lasted a second but promised a lifetime before she raced to her plane.

Reed waved her aloft.

Being Kathy Lee, when she waved back, it was with a slow waggle of the huge airplane's wings, because she never did anything by halves.

# DRONE (EXCERPT)

## IF YOU ENJOYED THAT, YOU'LL LOVE MIRANDA CHASE!

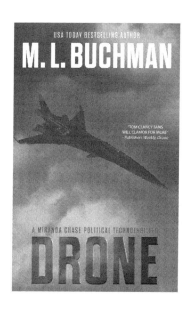

# DRONE (EXCERPT)

Flight 630 at 37,000 feet
12 nautical miles north of
Santa Fe, New Mexico, USA

THE FLIGHT ATTENDANT STEPPED UP TO HER SEAT—4E—which had never been her favorite on a 767-300. At least the cabin setup was in the familiar 261-seat, 2-class configuration, currently running at a seventy-three percent load capacity with a standard crew of ten and one ride-along FAA inspector in the cockpit jump seat.

"Excuse me, are you Miranda Chase?"

She nodded.

The attendant made a face that she couldn't interpret.

A frown? Did that indicate anger?

He turned away before she could consider the possibilities and, without another word, returned to his station at the front of the cabin.

Miranda once again straightened the emergency exit plan that the flight's vibrations kept shifting askew in its pocket.

This flight from yesterday's meeting at LAX to today's DC lunch meeting at the National Transportation Safety Board's headquarters departed so early that she'd decided to spend the night in the airline's executive lounge working on various aviation accident reports. She never slept on a flight and would have to catch up on her sleep tonight.

Miranda felt the shift as the plane turned into a modest five-degree bank to the left. The bright rays of dawn over the New Mexico desert shifted from the left-hand windows to the right side.

At due north, she heard the Rolls-Royce RB211 engines (quite a pleasant high tone compared to the Pratt & Whitney PW4000 that she always found unnerving) ease off ever so slightly, signaling a slow descent. The pilot was transitioning from an eastbound course that would be flown at an odd number of thousands of feet to a westbound one that must be flown at an even number.

The flight attendant then picked up the intercom phone and a loud squawk sounded through the cabin. Most people would be asleep and there were soft complaints and rustling down the length of the aircraft.

"We regret to inform you that there is an emergency on the ground. I repeat, there is nothing wrong with the plane. We are being routed back to Las Vegas, where we will disembark one passenger, refuel, and then continue our flight to DC. Our apologies for the inconvenience."

There were now shouts of complaint all up and down the aisle.

The flight attendant was staring straight at her as he slammed the intercom back into its cradle with significantly greater force than was required to seat it properly.

Oh. It was her they would be disembarking. That meant there was a crash in need of an NTSB investigator—a major one if they were flying back an hour in the wrong direction.

Thankfully, she always had her site kit with her.

For some reason, her seatmate was muttering something foul. Miranda ignored it and began to prepare herself.

Only the crash mattered.

She straightened the exit plan once more. It had shifted the other way with the changing harmonic from the RB211 engines.

———

## Chengdu, Central China

AIR FORCE MAJOR WANG FAN EASED BACK ON THE joystick of the final prototype Shenyang J-31 jet—designed exclusively for the People's Liberation Army Air Force. In response, China's newest fighter jet leapt upward like a catapult's missile from the PLAAF base in the flatlands surrounding the towering city of Chengdu.

It felt as he'd just been grasped by Chen Mei-Li. Never had a woman made him feel like such a man.

———

*Get* Drone *and fly into a whole series of action and danger! Available at fine retailers everywhere.*

*Drone*

# ABOUT THE AUTHOR

USA Today and Amazon #1 Bestseller M. L. "Matt" Buchman started writing on a flight south from Japan to ride his bicycle across the Australian Outback. Just part of a solo around-the-world trip that ultimately launched his writing career.

From the very beginning, his powerful female heroines insisted on putting character first, *then* a great adventure. He's since written over 60 action-adventure thrillers and military romantic suspense novels. And just for the fun of it: 100 short stories, and a fast-growing pile of read-by-author audiobooks.

Booklist says: "3X Top 10 of the Year." PW says: "Tom Clancy fans open to a strong female lead will clamor for more." His fans say: "I want more now...of everything." That his characters are even more insistent than his fans is a hoot.

As a 30-year project manager with a geophysics degree who has designed and built houses, flown and jumped out of planes, and solo-sailed a 50' ketch, he is awed by what is possible. More at: www. mlbuchman.com.

## Other works by M. L. Buchman: *(* - also in audio)*

### Action-Adventure Thrillers

#### Dead Chef
*One Chef!*
*Two Chef!*

#### Miranda Chase
*Drone\**
*Thunderbolt\**
*Condor\**
*Ghostrider\**
*Raider\**
*Chinook\**
*Havoc\**
*White Top\**

### Romantic Suspense

#### Delta Force
*Target Engaged\**
*Heart Strike\**
*Wild Justice\**
*Midnight Trust\**

#### Firehawks
**MAIN FLIGHT**
*Pure Heat*
*Full Blaze*
*Hot Point\**
*Flash of Fire\**
*Wild Fire*
**SMOKEJUMPERS**
*Wildfire at Dawn\**
*Wildfire at Larch Creek\**
*Wildfire on the Skagit\**

#### The Night Stalkers
**MAIN FLIGHT**
*The Night Is Mine*
*I Own the Dawn*
*Wait Until Dark*
*Take Over at Midnight*

*Light Up the Night*
*Bring On the Dusk*
*By Break of Day*
**AND THE NAVY**
*Christmas at Steel Beach*
*Christmas at Peleliu Cove*
**WHITE HOUSE HOLIDAY**
*Daniel's Christmas\**
*Frank's Independence Day\**
*Peter's Christmas\**
*Zachary's Christmas\**
*Roy's Independence Day\**
*Damien's Christmas\**
**5E**
*Target of the Heart*
*Target Lock on Love*
*Target of Mine*
*Target of One's Own*

#### Shadow Force: Psi
*At the Slightest Sound\**
*At the Quietest Word\**
*At the Merest Glance\**
*At the Clearest Sensation\**

#### White House Protection Force
*Off the Leash\**
*On Your Mark\**
*In the Weeds\**

### Contemporary Romance

#### Eagle Cove
*Return to Eagle Cove*
*Recipe for Eagle Cove*
*Longing for Eagle Cove*
*Keepsake for Eagle Cove*

#### Henderson's Ranch
*Nathan's Big Sky\**
*Big Sky, Loyal Heart\**
*Big Sky Dog Whisperer\**

# Other works by M. L. Buchman:

## Contemporary Romance (cont)

### Love Abroad
*Heart of the Cotswolds: England*
*Path of Love: Cinque Terre, Italy*

### Where Dreams
*Where Dreams are Born*
*Where Dreams Reside*
*Where Dreams Are of Christmas\**
*Where Dreams Unfold*
*Where Dreams Are Written*

## Science Fiction / Fantasy

### Deities Anonymous
*Cookbook from Hell: Reheated*
*Saviors 101*

### Single Titles
*The Nara Reaction*
*Monk's Maze*
*the Me and Elsie Chronicles*

## Non-Fiction

### Strategies for Success
*Managing Your Inner Artist/Writer*
*Estate Planning for Authors\**
*Character Voice*
*Narrate and Record Your Own*
*Audiobook\**

# Short Story Series by M. L. Buchman:

## Romantic Suspense

### Delta Force
*Th Delta Force Shooters*
*The Delta Force Warriors*

### Firehawks
*The Firehawks Lookouts*
*The Firehawks Hotshots*
*The Firebirds*

### The Night Stalkers
*The Night Stalkers 5D Stories*
*The Night Stalkers 5E Stories*
*The Night Stalkers CSAR*
*The Night Stalkers Wedding Stories*

### US Coast Guard

### White House Protection Force

## Contemporary Romance

### Eagle Cove

### Henderson's Ranch\*

### Where Dreams

## Action-Adventure Thrillers

### Dead Chef

### Miranda Chase Origin Stories

## Science Fiction / Fantasy

### Deities Anonymous

### Other
*The Future Night Stalkers*
*Single Titles*

# SIGN UP FOR M. L. BUCHMAN'S NEWSLETTER TODAY

*and receive:*
*Release News*
*Free Short Stories*
*a Free Book*

*Get your free book today. Do it now.*
*free-book.mlbuchman.com*

Printed in Great Britain
by Amazon

58652432R00038